This Walker book belongs to:

_____

_____

_____

First published 1986 by Walker Books Ltd
87 Vauxhall Walk, London SE11 5HJ

This edition published 2008

2 4 6 8 10 9 7 5 3

© 1986 Colin West

The right of Colin West to be identified as author/illustrator of this work has been asserted by him
in accordance with the Copyright, Designs and Patents Act 1988

This book has been typeset in Optima

Printed in China

British Library Cataloguing in Publication Data:
a catalogue record for this book is available from the British Library

ISBN 978-1-4063-2101-2

www.walker.co.uk

"Have you seen the crocodile?"

Colin West

WALKER BOOKS
AND SUBSIDIARIES
LONDON · BOSTON · SYDNEY · AUCKLAND

"Have you seen the crocodile?" asked the parrot.

"No,"
said the
dragonfly.

"Have you seen the crocodile?"
asked the parrot
and the dragonfly.

"No," said the bumble bee.

"Have you seen the crocodile?"
asked the parrot
and the dragonfly
and the bumble bee.

"No," said the butterfly.

"Have you seen the crocodile?"
asked the parrot
and the dragonfly
and the bumble bee
and the butterfly.

"No,"
said the
hummingbird.

"Have you seen the crocodile?"
asked the parrot
and the dragonfly
and the bumble bee
and the butterfly
and the hummingbird.

"No," said the frog.

"No one's seen the crocodile?"
  said the parrot
  and the dragonfly
  and the bumble bee
  and the butterfly
  and the hummingbird
  and the frog.

But then...

"Have YOU seen the parrot
and the dragonfly
and the bumble bee
and the butterfly
and the hummingbird
and the frog?"

asked the crocodile.

Colin West says of the last picture in *"Have You Seen the Crocodile?"*,
"The crocodile looks very pleased with himself, but I wonder
if all the other animals escaped being gobbled up?
In the previous picture, they seem to be doing a good job
of escaping! By the way, did you spot the little frog
hiding amongst the lily pads in the endpapers?"